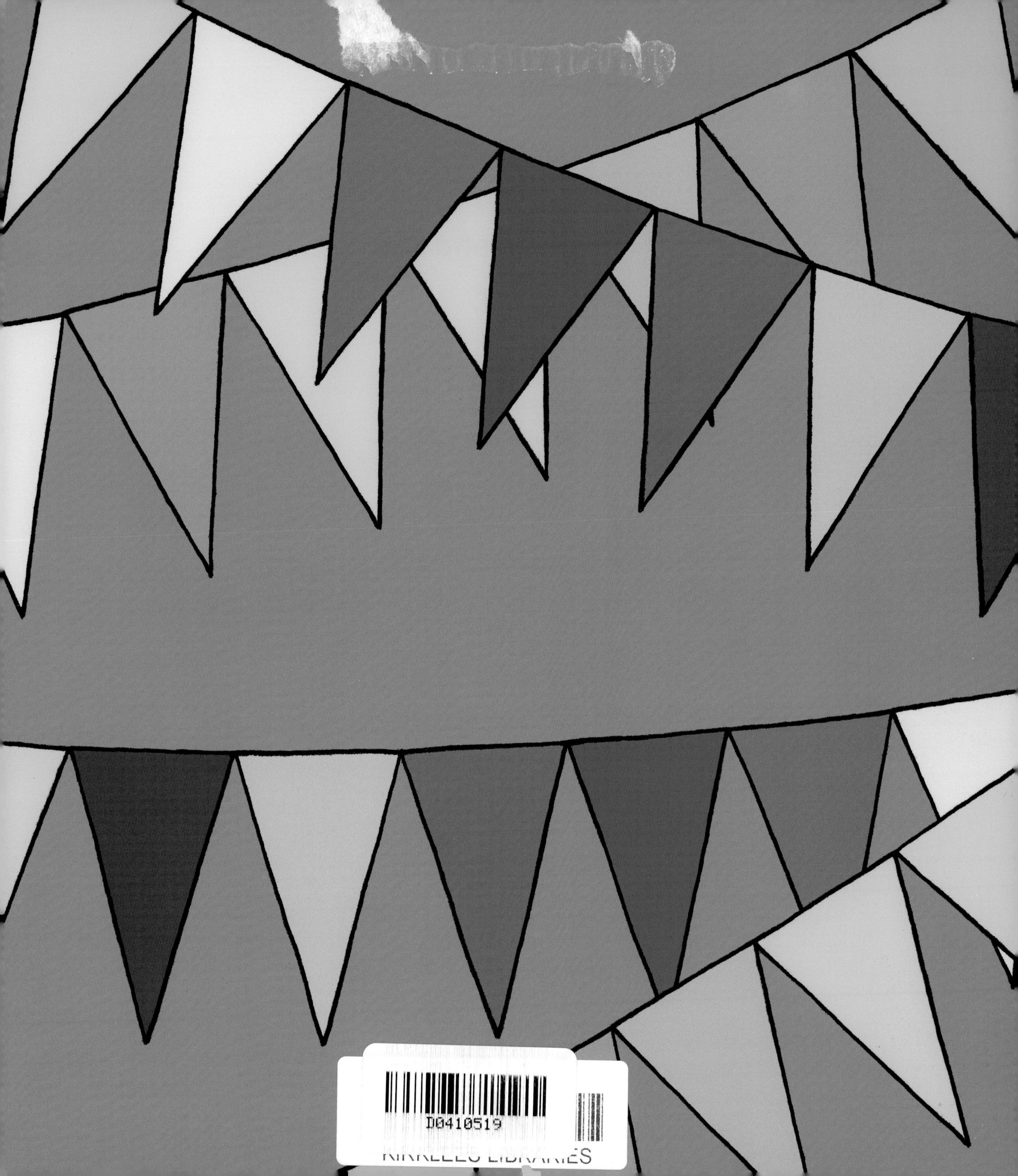

For Terry and Ana
NS

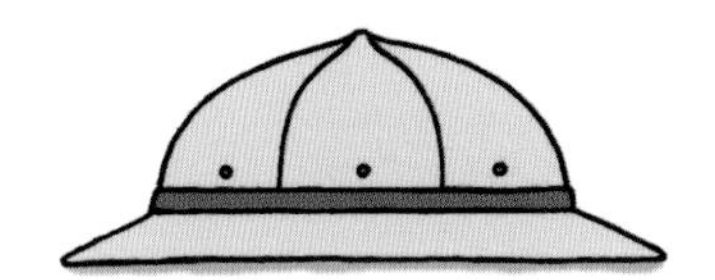

For Daisy and Harry
SS

First published 2010 by Walker Books Ltd, 87 Vauxhall Walk, London SE11 5HJ

2 4 6 8 10 9 7 5 3 1

This book has been typeset in Gill Sans

Printed in China

British Library Cataloguing in Publication Data:
a catalogue record for this book is available from the British Library

ISBN 978-1-4063-2619-2

www.walker.co.uk

Something beginning with BLUE

Nick Sharratt

Sally Symes

WALKER BOOKS
AND SUBSIDIARIES
LONDON • BOSTON • SYDNEY • AUCKLAND

I spy with my little eye,

something beginning with …

blue.

It isn't blue sky and it isn't blue sea.

It's five hundred and fifty times

bigger than me…

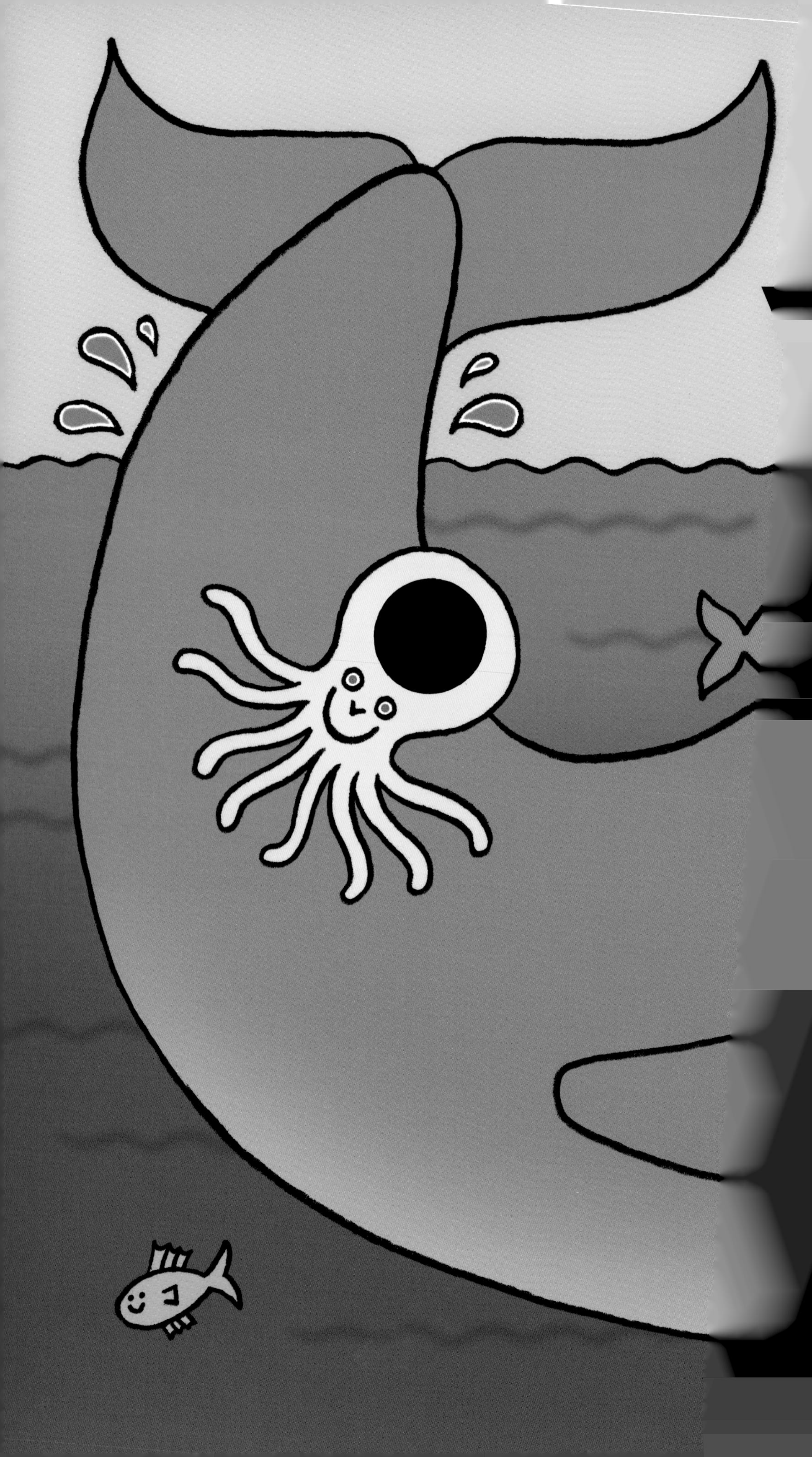

I spy with my little eye,

something beginning with ...

green.

It's not one of these

and it's not one of those.

It's got tough, scaly skin and blows

smoke through its nose...

A green
dragon!

I spy with my little eye,

something beginning with …

grey.

It doesn't eat cheese.

It might like some hay.

If it started to **charge**

I'd get out of the way (fast!)…

A grey rhinoceros!

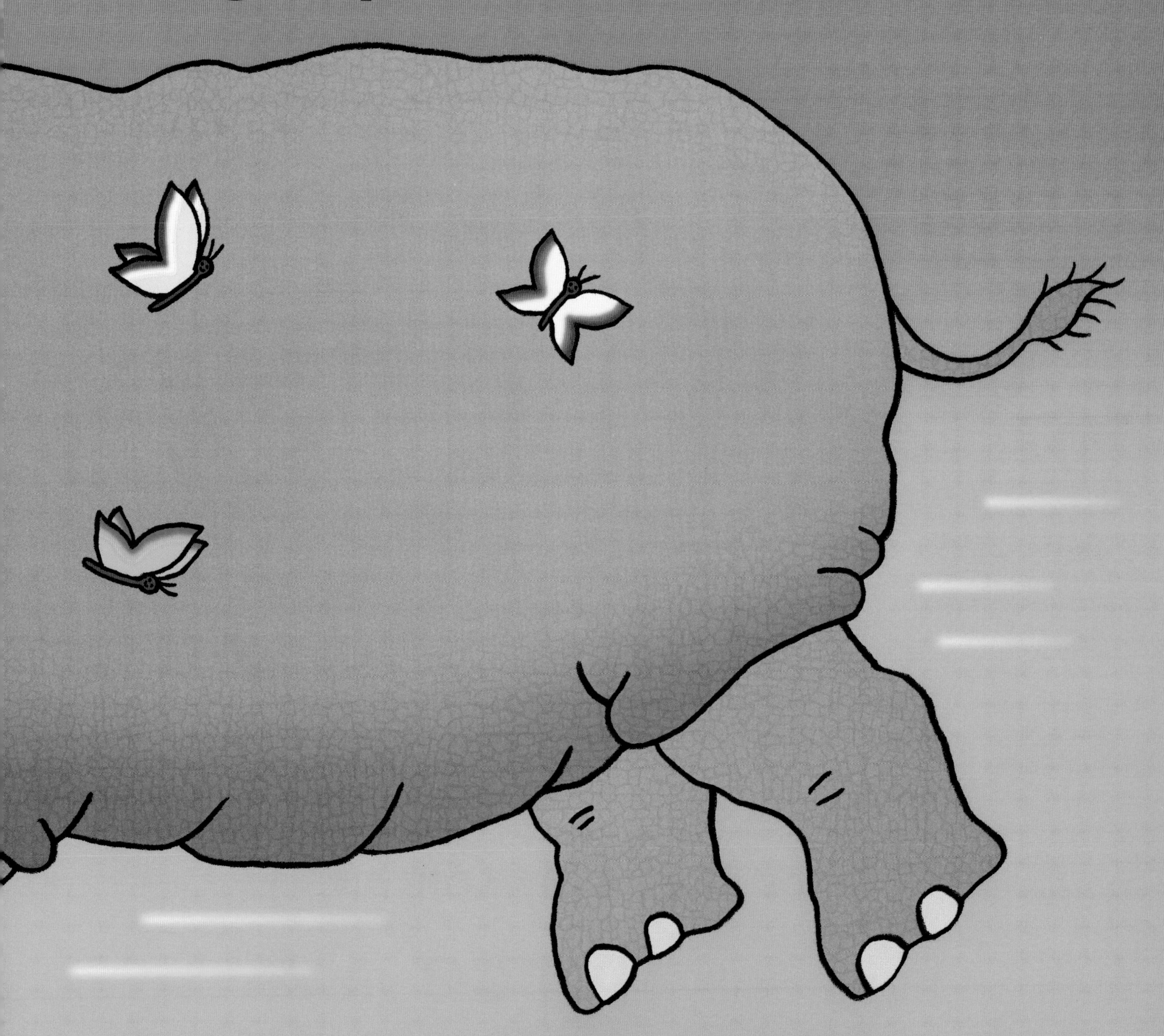

I spy with my little eye,

something beginning with …

brown.

It's not chocolate buttons.

It's not a brown owl.

It's got lovely soft fur,

but a really **fierce** growl…

RAAARGH!

A brown **bear!**

I spy with my little eye,

something beginning with …

black.

It's not a black bird.

It's not a black cat.

It has eight wriggling legs

and is hairy and **fat**…

A black spider!

We spy with our little eyes,

something beginning with …

yummy!

It's

bursting with all of

the **colours** you see…

Can you guess
what it is?

It's our
fancy
dress
tea!